A PERFECT DAY

jennifer
yerkes

EERDMANS BOOKS FOR YOUNG READERS

GRAND RAPIDS, MICHIGAN

The day begins
in peaceful harmony.

Chirp-chirp!
Chirp!

Cree-cree!

Cree-cree!
Creeee!

Bzzz-zzz! Zzz-zzz!

Croa-oak!
Croa-oak!

Whoosh!
Whoosh!

Ssss . . . sss . . .
Ssss . . . ssss . . . sss . . .

Rah-rah!
Rah!

The melody continues
throughout the day.

Suddenly,
the drums begin
to roll.

The cymbals crash!

And the maracas
mark the rhythm.